MANNERS
MAKETH
MOUSE
(AND EVERYONE ELSE)

MISS MOLLY'S
SCHOOL OF MANNERS

Pleased to meet you. Do come in.

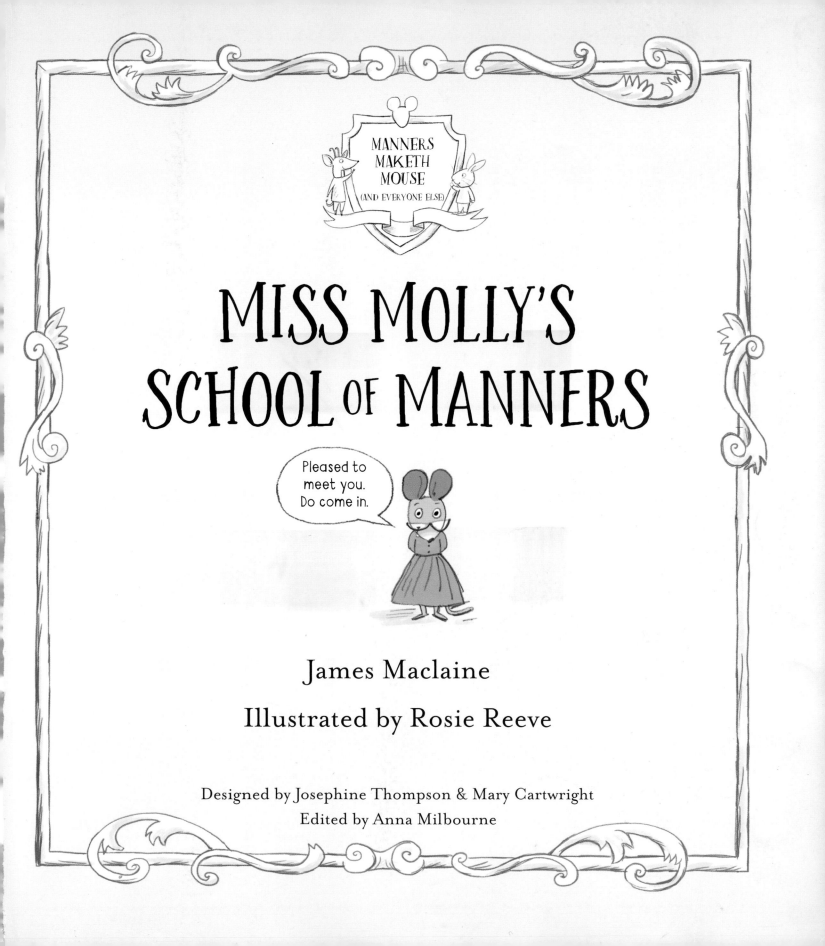

James Maclaine

Illustrated by Rosie Reeve

Designed by Josephine Thompson & Mary Cartwright
Edited by Anna Milbourne

This is the story of a little raccoon
named Algernon, and how the events
of one strange day made his
BAD manners GOOD.

A lgernon's manners weren't just bad – they were terrible!

He never said please.

He never said thank you.

He didn't think to help others.

He didn't bother saying sorry.

In short, Algernon cared for no one but himself, until, one morning, he stumbled upon

a rather

unusual

place…

Miss Molly took Algernon into her school. "Please join us," she said, "and you'll soon learn how good manners can make life better for everyone."

Just then, two eager beavers appeared, spouting polite words but barging down the stairs to greet Miss Molly.

"Good manners aren't just about using the right words," Miss Molly remarked. "They're about showing you care."

HISTORY OF MANNERS

Ps & Qs PRACTICE ROOM

MEET OUR STAFF

Mr. Even-Stevens
Professor Goggles
Miss Molly
Sir Lionel
Ms. Klaxon
Madame Merci-Beaucoup

Herr Sourschnapp
Dr. Almanac
School Nurse
Signor Leopardo
Mrs. Buttersoft

Ooof!

Good morning, Miss Molly.

Excuse me! Thank you! Please!

Ow!

Rude noises were coming from the Listening Carefully Lab, where the first lesson had already begun...

7

Oh dear! An experiment had just exploded because a polar bear hadn't been paying attention.

Professor Goggles sighed. "It's good manners to listen carefully when someone explains something to you. I'll say it again – if your experiment makes rude noises, add a sprinkle of Pardon Me Powder."

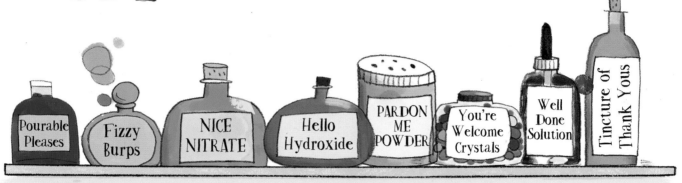

Pourable Pleases

Fizzy Burps

NICE NITRATE

Hello Hydroxide

PARDON ME POWDER

You're Welcome Crystals

Well Done Solution

Tincture of Thank Yous

Algernon wanted to have a turn too.

Which of the chemicals on the shelf should you add to this burping flask?

BELCH
BURP

He chose the orange container and the flask stopped burping. "Well done," said Miss Molly.

The next lesson was in the Sharing Studio. Algernon and two others in the class were supposed to paint a tiger. Agatha Aardvark grabbed the red paint, and Algernon seized the yellow, but neither was happy. "There's no orange paint!" Algernon complained.

Luckily, Signor Leopardo taught them the fine art of sharing. "You'll have to share red and yellow," he told them. "Mixing them together makes orange!"

Rembrandt van Rhino

Vincent van Goat

Catavaggio

And if you all share the black paint...

...we could all add stripes.

"Sharing doesn't just mean giving and getting," Miss Molly added. "It also means taking turns and leaving enough for others…"

"However, some things, and some opinions, are best kept to yourself."

For her conversation class, Madame Merci-Beaucoup asked the animals to talk about their hobbies. Nobody got a chance to speak at first because a rabbit talked on and on…

Tina Turtle was too scared to take part until a considerate giraffe brought her out of her shell.

"You should always think about who you're talking to," Madame Merci-Beaucoup advised. "Speak clearly so they can hear you…"

"…BUT not too loudly of course."

"Was it necessary to shout?" Miss Molly asked.
"Definitely not!" said Algernon, who had learned another lesson.

It was time for everyone to go outside to play.

Two animals sat unhappily on the swings. They weren't able to swing until one of them had a bright idea.

When the mice lost their ball they knew how to use good manners to get it back.

Algernon barged wildly into a game, knocking everything down and upsetting the players.

"But I wanted to play!" he protested.
"Perhaps you could ask to join in next time," suggested Miss Molly.
"Watch how Edith Elephant does it…"

Asking nicely worked for Algernon too. He had fun with the others before Miss Molly announced: "Lunchtime!"

Miss Molly led Algernon into the Dining Hall of Decorum. He waited patiently, but then Mrs. Buttersoft, the cook, tried to serve him some cauliflower. "Yuck! I hate cauliflower!" Algernon blurted.

Mrs. Buttersoft was upset. Her tears dripped into the roast potatoes, turning them soggy.

NEITHER BURPING NOR SLURPING

MRS. BUTTERSOFT'S BUFFET

You hurt her feelings. Just say, "No thank you," instead.

Bad manners spoiled the taste of several meals on the other side of the room, too…

After lunch, Algernon felt confused – his head was a jumble of manners. When the next teacher, Mr. Even-Stevens, gave him some worksheets to do, Algernon didn't know what to say…

Still, he did his best to answer all the questions, and then Mr. Even-Stevens checked them.

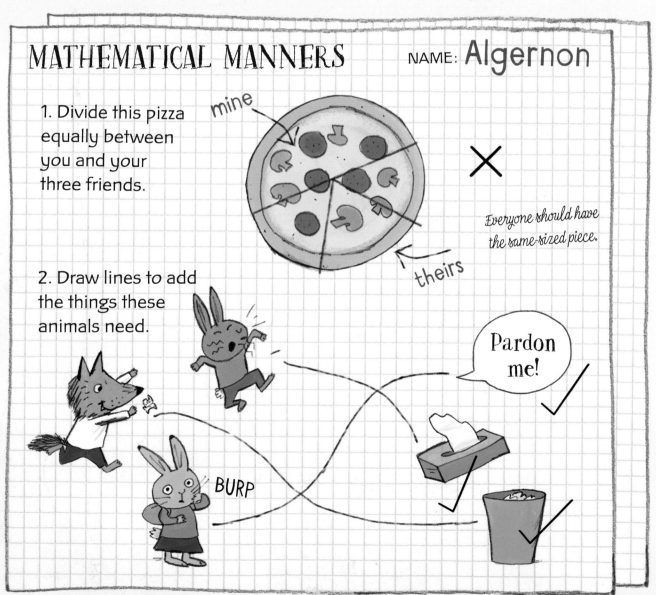

MATHEMATICAL MANNERS   NAME: Algernon

1. Divide this pizza equally between you and your three friends.

mine

theirs

Everyone should have the same-sized piece.

2. Draw lines to add the things these animals need.

Pardon me!

BURP

18

3. Take away the bad manners. On each picture, circle what needs to be removed.

You need to take away the headphones when someone is talking to you!

4. Draw hands on the clock to show when you'd arrive to meet someone at three o'clock.

But it's even better to arrive a few minutes early.

SCORE: 6/8

Well done, Algernon – you're making good progress.

19

Next came the History of Manners lesson with Sir Lionel. "Bad manners have often caused bad things to happen – as you can see on this tapestry," he began.

BAD MANNERS TAPESTRY

1. IN THE YEAR 1066, AN UNRULY MOB SAILED TO A FARAWAY LAND.

2. THERE, THEY ARGUED ABOUT WHO SHOULD BE KING.

3. SO THE BATTLE OF HATINGS BROKE OUT.

4. AT LAST, THEY AGREED TO TAKE TURNS BEING KING INSTEAD.

"Long ago, knights thought that obeying kings and rescuing damsels in distress were good manners," Sir Lionel continued. "Why don't you give them a try and see what you think?"

Kill the dragon!

AAAAARGH!!

There's no need to threaten me. I'll let you pass if you say please.

"I don't even need rescuing. Damsels can help themselves nowadays, thank you," tutted Jessie Jaguar. "These manners are out of date!"

"But it's STILL polite to offer help to anyone in need," said Miss Molly.

Um... I can't get down!

Algernon to the rescue!

"Some good manners are correct for some occasions, and not for others," explained Dr. Almanac in the Ps and Qs Practice Room. "Why don't you try greeting the Queen, then a friend's parents? You can find a few tips on my courtesy cards."

A friendly fox was a little TOO friendly...

Hi Queenie, darling.

COURTESY CARD No. 1

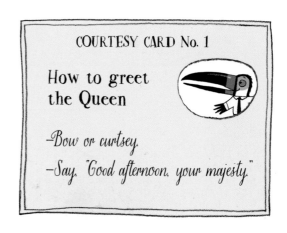

How to greet the Queen

—Bow or curtsey.

—Say, "Good afternoon, your majesty."

And the eager beavers overdid it again...

It's our privilege to meet you, your excellencies.

COURTESY CARD No. 2

How to greet a friend's parents

—No need for bowing or scraping.

—Smile and say, "Nice to meet you."

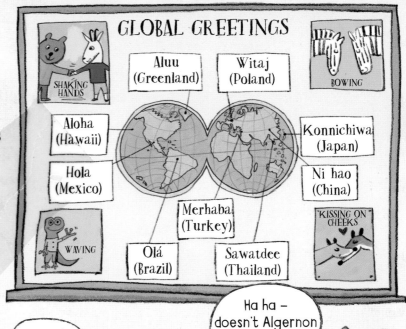

GLOBAL GREETINGS

SHAKING HANDS

BOWING

Aluu (Greenland)

Witaj (Poland)

Aloha (Hawaii)

Konnichiwa (Japan)

Hola (Mexico)

Ni hao (China)

Merhaba (Turkey)

KISSING ON CHEEKS

WAVING

Olá (Brazil)

Sawatdee (Thailand)

Dr. Almanac then taught the class lots of different ways of saying hello around the world.

The animals bowed, shook hands and waved, but when Algernon tried to greet someone with a kiss, Ernest Otter teased him.

Mwa!

Ha ha – doesn't Algernon look silly?

Miss Molly came to the rescue as Algernon began to cry. "Let's see if we can help you feel better in the Sorry Sick Bay," she said.

23

Algernon and Ernest had to wait in the Sorry Sick Bay until the School Nurse had finished her rounds.

First she treated Mitzi Monkey and Hector Hippo, whose hot tempers had caused an argument.

Two ill-mannered animals had been in a fight. They also hurt on the inside because they'd called each other names.

Next, she smoothed a parrot's feathers, which a nosy friend had ruffled.

At last, the School Nurse reached Algernon and Ernest. "There's no use hiding," she said. "Come out and say sorry – this is my prescription for a proper apology…"

Apology x 1

Admit you did something wrong.

Say it with meaning – no silly voices.

Don't forget to use the words, "I am sorry".

And if someone says sorry to you properly, try to listen and accept the apology.

Signed: *The School Nurse*

After following the Nurse's advice, Ernest and Algernon both felt better. "Sorry is a useful word," said Miss Molly. "Follow me and we'll find some more…"

So, Miss Molly took Algernon to the Library of Lovely Language. Here Miss Molly's students looked up polite phrases in the dictionaries and learned which words to use when.

"Some things are best left unsaid," whispered the School Librarian, who was returning an encyclopedia of insults to the Secret Archive.

One book that Miss Molly showed Algernon was called 'Bravos for Beginners'. "You can use some of these words next," she said. "Did I tell you it was Good Sports Day this afternoon?"

27

Down on the sports field, some of the animals forgot their sporting manners. Zita Cheetah wasn't playing fair, so Ms. Klaxon blew her whistle. "Good sports don't cheat!" she said.

GOOD SPORTS DAY

"Now before you jump, please check that the way is clear," warned Signor Leopardo... a little too late.

WHEEE!

WHEEE!

OUCH!

Sir Lionel encouraged a few supporters who'd given up. "Keep cheering," he said. "Show your team that you care."

After the tug of war, both winners and losers needed words of advice. "Gloating wins you no friends," said Mr. Even-Stevens. "And grumbling doesn't change a thing," said the School Nurse.

BUT, although Algernon was on the losing side, his winning manners impressed Miss Molly.

Home time had come for Algernon.

"You've done very well today,
Algernon," said Miss Molly.
"Thank you," Algernon beamed.
"Shall I come back tomorrow?"

"There's no need," replied Miss Molly.
"Keep in mind everything you've
learned here and you'll be fine."

MISS MOLLY'S
SCHOOL
OF
MANNERS

Goodbye,
Algernon!

Goodbye,
Miss Molly!

Algernon didn't come across Miss Molly's school ever again. But he never forgot the lessons he'd learned there. And life was certainly better for Algernon – and everyone who met him – now that he had good manners.

MISS MOLLY'S SCHOOL OF MANNERS

Thank you.
Miss Molly.

Love.
Algernon